DEDICATION

The legacy and life of Francis Carroll Wilson Sr. The quiet, soft-spoken, gentle horseman whose face was seen around the world for over forty years. Those that knew Francis simply called him Frank. You would often see Frank show his horsemanship across the media, whether it be on the front of a magazine, newspaper, or on television showcasing his professionalism by posing some of the world's most valuable thoroughbreds.

This book is also dedicated to all past, present, and future Frankie's Corner Little Thoroughbred Crusade students. Continue to dream BIG, only you can stop yourself from being the best version of yourself. With hard work and dedication, you can achieve anything you put your mind to!

www.FRANKIESCORNER.org

"Max, what do you say buddy, let's take you to run in the derby," said Frankie. Max replied, "I'm a quarter horse not a thoroughbred."
"If you agree I'll be your jockey", said Frankie. Max laughs at Frankie.

"Anything you put your mind to, you can achieve it". "All we must do is plan and stick to the plan", said Frankie.

Frankie and Max sat on a bale of hay thinking of a way they could compete with the thoroughbred.

Frankie and Max went to the training center and hid behind a tree to watch how the thoroughbreds trained. Frankie encouraged Max as he jumped up and down. "We can do this Max; we can do it!" "Ok, I'm going to trust you Frankie", said Max in an unsure voice.

"We have seven months to make it happen." First, we must get up and run every day. Each day we must push ourselves harder than the day before. Max's eye got big as he said, "I don't think I can do this".

"We can do this Max!" Frankie uplifted Max by telling him "we are a team; I will be with you every step of the way!" Anything you put your mind to, you can achieve it!

The next morning Frankie went to Max's Stall to find that Max was still snoozing." Good morning Max, it is a beautiful morning for our first workout." "Frankie, I don't think I can do this", said Max. Remember, anything you put your mind to, you can achieve it! Okay Frankie!

For the next five months Max and Frankie woke up every morning at 4:00 am to train. They trained seven days a week. Each day they would run up and down the hills of the pastures on the farm, ending their training with a 300-yard sprint to the pond for a drink of water.

"Frankie, I'm feeling Great!!!" "I've got my wind; my legs feel great! I think I'm ready to train with the thoroughbreds", said Max!

That is a great idea Max! "For our last two months of training we will do just that, train with the thoroughbreds," said Frankie.

The next morning Max was so excited to train with the thoroughbreds, that he went to Frankie's window to wake him up earlier than normal.

Max and Frankie arrived at the training track around 5:00 am to find that the thoroughbreds were already training on the track.

"Hey fatty, what are you doing here"? "This is the thoroughbreds training track, no fat quarter horses allowed", said a chestnut thoroughbred. Let's go Frankie, let's get out of here!!! Max and Frankie started walking away.

"Hey Boys" a female voiced yelled. Hi, my name is Anya', I'm a trainer here at the track, what are you two doing here?" "We are here to train for the derby", said Frankie. "You two do know that the derby is in two months and it's a little late to be training", said Anya'. "Yes, ma'am we have been training at the farm for the last five months", said Frankie.

"Well boys, I have an idea", said Ms. Anya. The two of you can come over to my track at Reese Farm to train for the next two months." Thank you so much Ms. Anya, "Max and I really appreciate you", said Frankie!

For the next two month's Frankie and Max trained at Anya's farm. Each day Frankie and Max trained to see how fast they could run 14 furlongs to challenge themselves.

One week before the big race, Anya' went to the track while drinking her morning tea to watch Frankie and Max train. You two look great, but may I ask why your running 14 furlongs, the race is only 10 furlongs.

Frankie and Max looked at each other and laughed. "Well Ms. Anya', I guess we are over prepared!" All three laughed hysterically.

It's the day of the big race. Frankie and Max were so nervous they got to the Derby stadium before all the other horses. Remember Max, anything you put your mind to, you can achieve it.

6

The horn sounded for the call to post and the announcer said loudly "Riders up" over PA system.

Frankie and Max loaded in the number 7 starting gate with their orange and purple silks.

"Look boys, fatty really showed up to race with us thoroughbreds", said the chestnut colored horse in the number 1 loading gate. "I hope he is ready to eat my dust", said another horse.

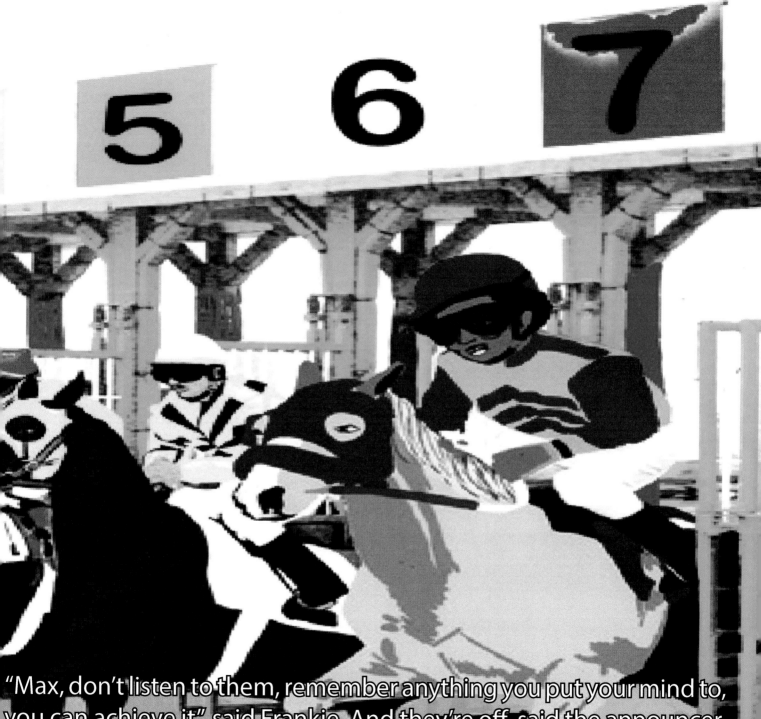

"Max, don't listen to them, remember anything you put your mind to, you can achieve it", said Frankie. And they're off, said the announcer. Frankie and Max come out of the gates in last place.

Rounding the second turn on the back stretch, the boys were still in last place. "Remember all of our training Max. We ran the hills on the farm to get our legs in shape for today, we are on flat ground now", it is time to show them what we are made of, said Frankie with confidence in his voice.

"Hold on Frankie", said Max. "Let's show these thoroughbreds what this quarter horse is made of." Max put his gallop in to overdrive passing four thoroughbreds.

Woohoo yelled Frankie!!! Go little buddy go!! You’re doing AMAZNG!!! You can do it Max!!!

7 furlongs left in the race, Frankie yells to Max, Believe…. Achieve!!!!! To Max's every stride BELIEVE, ACHIEVE, BELIEVE, ACHIEVE, BELIEVE, ACHIEVE…….

Frankie and Max charge between the final two horses to win the Derby by 3 horse length.

With the trainer Anya'Frankie and MAX stand in the winner's celebrating the win. "I bet those thoroughbreds won't talk about another chubby quarter horse again", said Max. Frankie replies, "anything you believe you can achieve!!"

71992169R00022